Dear Parent:
Your child's love of reading starts here!

Every child learns to read in a different way and at his or her own speed. Some go back and forth between reading levels and read favorite books again and again. Others read through each level in order. You can help your young reader improve and become more confident by encouraging his or her own interests and abilities. From books your child reads with you to the first books he or she reads alone, there are I Can Read Books for every stage of reading:

SHARED READING
Basic language, word repetition, and whimsical illustrations, ideal for sharing with your emergent reader

BEGINNING READING
Short sentences, familiar words, and simple concepts for children eager to read on their own

READING WITH HELP
Engaging stories, longer sentences, and language play for developing readers

READING ALONE
Complex plots, challenging vocabulary, and high-interest topics for the independent reader

ADVANCED READING
Short paragraphs, chapters, and exciting themes for the perfect bridge to chapter books

I Can Read Books have introduced children to the joy of reading since 1957. Featuring award-winning authors and illustrators and a fabulous cast of beloved characters, I Can Read Books set the standard for beginning readers.

A lifetime of discovery begins with the magical words "I Can Read!"

Visit www.icanread.com for information
on enriching your child's reading experience.

HarperCollins*Publishers*

A BARGAIN FOR FRANCES

by Russell Hoban

Pictures by Lillian Hoban

A Bargain for Frances Text copyright © 1970 by Russell C. Hoban Illustrations copyright © 1970, 1992 by Lillian Hoban All rights reserved. No part of this book may be used or reproduced in any manner whatsoever without written permission except in the case of brief quotations embodied in critical articles and reviews. Printed in the United States of America. For information address HarperCollins Children's Books, a division of HarperCollins Publishers, 10 East 53rd Street, New York, NY 10022. www.harpercollinschildrens.com

Library of Congress Cataloging-in-Publication Data

Hoban, Russell.
  A bargain for Frances / by Russell Hoban ; pictures by Lillian Hoban.
    p.   cm. — (An I can read book)
  Summary: Thelma usually outsmarts Frances until Frances decides to teach her a lesson about friendship.
  ISBN-10: 0-06-022329-4 (trade bdg.) — ISBN-13: 978-0-06-022329-8 (trade bdg.)
  ISBN-10: 0-06-022330-8 (lib. bdg.) — ISBN-13: 978-0-06-022330-4 (lib. bdg.)
  ISBN-10: 0-06-444001-X (pbk.) — ISBN-13: 978-0-06-444001-1 (pbk.)
  [1. Badgers—Fiction. 2. Friendship—Fiction.] I. Hoban, Lillian, ill. II. Title. III. Series.
PZ7.H637Bar 1992   91-12267
[E]—dc20   CIP
                                                                                                                 AC

❖

13 LP/WOR 20 19 18 17 16 15 14 13 12 11

For Phoebe, Brom, Esmé, and Julia

It was a fine summer day,

and after breakfast Frances said,

"I am going to play with Thelma."

"Be careful," said Mother.

"Why do I have to be careful?"
said Frances.

"Remember the last time?" said Mother.

"Which time was that?" said Frances.

"That was the time you played catch

with Thelma's new boomerang,"
said Mother. "Thelma did
all the throwing, and you came home
with lumps on your head."
"I remember that time now,"
said Frances.

"And do you remember the other time
last winter?" said Mother.
"I remember that time too,"
said Frances.

"That was the first time
there was ice on the pond.
Thelma wanted to go skating,
and she told me
to try the ice first."
"Who came home wet?" said Mother.
"You or Thelma?"
"I came home wet," said Frances.

"Yes," said Mother.

"That is why I say be careful.

Because when you play with Thelma

you always get the worst of it."

"Well," said Frances, "this time

I do not have to be careful.

We are not playing with boomerangs.

We are not skating.

We are having a tea party,

and we are making a mud cake."

"Be careful anyhow," said Mother.

"All right," said Frances.

Frances took her dolls
to Thelma's house.
She took her alligator doll
and her elephant doll.
She took her snake doll
and her teddy bear too.

As Frances walked to Thelma's house
she sang:

> Alligators, bears and me
> Are very fond of drinking tea.
> The elephant and the wiggly snake
> Are happy when they eat their cake.

15

Frances and Thelma made a mud cake.

They put daisies on it for frosting.

Then Thelma got out her dolls

and her tea set.

"I am saving up
for a tea set," said Frances.
"I am saving all my allowances."
"This is the best kind to get,"
said Thelma. "It is plastic,
and it has red flowers on it."

"This is not the kind I want,"
said Frances.
"I want a real china tea set
with pictures on it in blue.
The tea set I want has trees
and birds and a Chinese house
and a fence and a boat
and people walking on a bridge.
I used to have
that kind of tea set.
But all I have now
is part of the teapot.
The rest of it is broken."

"That is why that kind
of tea set is no good,"
said Thelma. "The cups break
and the saucers break
and the teapot and cream pitcher
and sugar bowl break,
and then the set is all gone.
My tea set has red flowers,

and it does not break

unless you step on it."

"Well," said Frances, "I am saving up

for the other kind."

"How much have you saved up?"

said Thelma.

"Two dollars and seventeen cents,"

said Frances.

"How much does the tea set cost?"
said Thelma.

"I don't know,"
said Frances.

"I am sure they cost a lot,"
said Thelma.

"It will take you a long time
to save up all that money."

"I know," said Frances, "and I wish
I had a tea set now."

"Maybe I will sell you mine,"
said Thelma.

"I don't want yours," said Frances.
"I want a real china one
with pictures on it in blue."

"I don't think
they make them anymore,"
said Thelma. "I know another girl
who saved up for that tea set.
Her mother went to every store
and could not find one.

Then that girl lost

some of her money

and spent the rest on candy.

She never got the tea set.

This is what happens.

A lot of girls

never do get tea sets.

So maybe you won't get one."

25

"If I buy yours, I will
have a tea set," said Frances.

"You said you didn't want it,"
said Thelma. "And anyhow,
I don't want to sell it now."
"Why not?" said Frances.
"Well," said Thelma,
"it is a very good tea set.
It is plastic that does not break.
It has pretty red flowers on it.
It has all the cups and saucers.
It has the sugar bowl
and the cream pitcher and the teapot.
It is almost new, and I think
it cost a lot of money."

"I have two dollars

and seventeen cents," said Frances.

"That's a lot of money."

"I don't know," said Thelma.

"If I sell you my tea set,

then I won't have one anymore."

"We can have tea parties

at my house then," said Frances.

"And you can use the money

for a new doll."

"Well, maybe," said Thelma.

"Do you have your money with you?"

"I'll run home for it," said Frances.

"All right," said Thelma.

"I will think about it

while you run home for your money."

29

Frances ran home for her money.

When she came back, Thelma said,

"I will sell you my tea set."

Frances gave Thelma her money.

Thelma gave Frances her tea set.

"No backsies on this," said Thelma.

"All right," said Frances.

"No backsies."

Frances went home with her tea set and her dolls, and she sang:

A plastic pot can pour the tea

For my dolls and friends and me

Just as well as china.

Red is just as good as blue.

Plastic cups are all right too,

Just as good as china.

When Frances got home,
she showed the tea set
to her little sister Gloria.
"That is a very ugly tea set,"
said Gloria.
"What's the matter with it?"
said Frances.

"It's ugly," said Gloria.

"It's a nice tea set," said Frances.

"It's plastic," said Gloria.

"It has red flowers. It's ugly.
I like the china kind
with the pictures all in blue."

"You can't get that kind anymore,"

said Frances.

"They don't have them in the stores."

"Yes, they do," said Gloria.

"They have them now

at the candy store. My friend Ida

got one yesterday, and she showed it

to Thelma. So Thelma knows

they have them at the candy store.

They cost two dollars

and seven cents."

Frances walked slowly

to the candy store.

She looked inside,

and there was Thelma.

Thelma gave the storekeeper her money.

The storekeeper gave Thelma
a china tea set
with pictures all in blue.
Thelma did not see Frances
as Frances walked away.

Frances sang a little song

as she walked away:

Now that plastic's what I've got,

Backsies are what there is not.

Mother told me to be careful,

But Thelma better be bewareful.

Frances thought about no backsies
all the way home.

When she got home she put

a penny in the plastic sugar bowl

of her tea set.

Then she called Thelma

on the telephone.

"Hello," said Thelma.

"Hello," said Frances.

"This is Frances."

"Remember," said Thelma,

"no backsies."

"I remember," said Frances.

"But are you sure

you really want no backsies?"

"Sure I'm sure," said Thelma.

"You mean I never have to give back the tea set?" said Frances.

"That's right," said Thelma.

"You can keep the tea set."

"Can I keep what is in the sugar bowl too?" said Frances.

"What is in the sugar bowl?" said Thelma.

"Never mind," said Frances.

"No backsies. Good-bye."

Frances hung up.

Frances waited for the telephone
to ring, and when it rang
she said, "Hello."
"Hello," said Thelma.
"This is Thelma."
"I know," said Frances.

"I just remembered," said Thelma,

"I think I had something

in the sugar bowl.

I think it was a ring.

Did you find a ring?"

"No," said Frances. "And I don't have

to tell you what is in the sugar bowl

because you said no backsies."

"Well," said Thelma,

"I just remembered

that I put some money

in the sugar bowl one time.

I think it was some birthday money.

I think it was two dollars,

or maybe it was five dollars.

Did you find money?"

"You said no backsies," said Frances.

"So I don't have to tell you.

I don't have to say how much money
is in the sugar bowl."

"Well," said Thelma, "it is my money,
and I want it."

"Do you want backsies?" said Frances.

"Do you want your tea set back
and you will give my money back?"
"I can't," said Thelma,
"because I used the money
for a new tea set.
There is only a dime left over.
I will give you
the new tea set and the dime.
The new tea set is
the china kind you want.
It has pictures all in blue."
"You said they don't make that kind
anymore," said Frances.

"This one was very hard to find,"
said Thelma. "And I think it was
the very last one in the store."
"All right," said Frances.
"Bring it over."

Thelma brought over the china tea set
and the dime, and Frances gave back
the plastic tea set.

Then Thelma took the lid
off the sugar bowl
and saw the penny.

"That is not a very nice trick
to play on a friend," said Thelma.

52

"No," said Frances, "it is not.
And that was not a nice trick
you played on me
when you sold me your tea set."

"Well," said Thelma, "from now on
I will have to be careful
when I play with you."

"Being careful is not as much fun
as being friends," said Frances.
"Do you want to be careful,
or do you want to be friends?"

"I want to be friends," said Thelma.

"All right," said Frances.

"Then I will give you
halfies on the dime."

Frances and Thelma went
to the candy store with the dime.
Frances bought bubble gum,
and Thelma bought Life Savers.

Then they went back to Frances's house
to skip rope. Gloria came out
to turn the rope and skip too.

"You and Gloria can skip first,"
said Frances to Thelma.
"I will go last."

Thelma skipped first, then Gloria.

Then Frances skipped, and she sang:

> One for plastic, two for china,
>
> Three for yours and four for mine-a,
>
> Five for tea and six for cakes,
>
> Seven for elephants, eight for snakes,
>
> Nine's a trip to the candy store,
>
> Then comes ten and ten skips more:
>
> Backsies one, backsies two,
>
> Backsies are no fun to do.
>
> Careful once, careful twice,
>
> Being careful isn't nice.
>
> Being friends is better.

Then Frances and Thelma
shared their bubble gum
and Life Savers with Gloria.